GOOD FAMILIES DON'T

Story by Robert Munsch

Art by Alan Daniel

Doubleday Canada Limited, Toronto

Canadian Cataloguing in Publication Data

Munsch, Robert N., 1945-
Good families don't

ISBN 0-385-25267-6

I. Daniel, Alan, 1939-   . II. Title.

PS8576.U58G66 1990   jC813'.54   C90-094231-2
PZ7.M86Go 1990

Typeset by Southam Business Information and
Communications Group Inc.
Cover Design: Tania Craan
Film: Colour Technologies
Editorial, production
and design manager:
Maggie Reeves

Published in Canada by
Doubleday Canada Ltd.
105 Bond Street
Toronto, Ontario
M5B 1Y3

Printed and bound in the USA

To Carmen
To Joseph

One night
Carmen
walked
up the stairs
to her bedroom.

There, lying on her bed,
was a great big purple,
green and yellow fart.

She
ran
down
the stairs
yelling,

"Mommy-Daddy!
Mommy-Daddy!
Mommy-Daddy!
There is a fart
up on my bed."

"Don't be ridiculous!" said her father.
"Good families like ours do not have farts."
Nevertheless, he walked up the stairs
to see what was going on.

When he opened the door to the bedroom,
the fart jumped on him.
He said, "Awk! Glach! Argggg!"
and fell right on down.

After a while Carmen began to wonder how her father was doing. She crawled up the stairs very slowly, looked over the top step and saw her father's feet sticking out from underneath the fart.

So Carmen
ran downstairs
yelling,

"Mommy, Mommy, Mommy!
There is a fart
on top of Daddy!"

"Don't be ridiculous," said the mother.
"Good families like ours do not have farts. What
would the neighbors say?" Nevertheless, she went
upstairs to see what was going on. She opened
the door and the fart jumped on her. She said,
"Awk! Glach! Argggg!" and fell right on down.

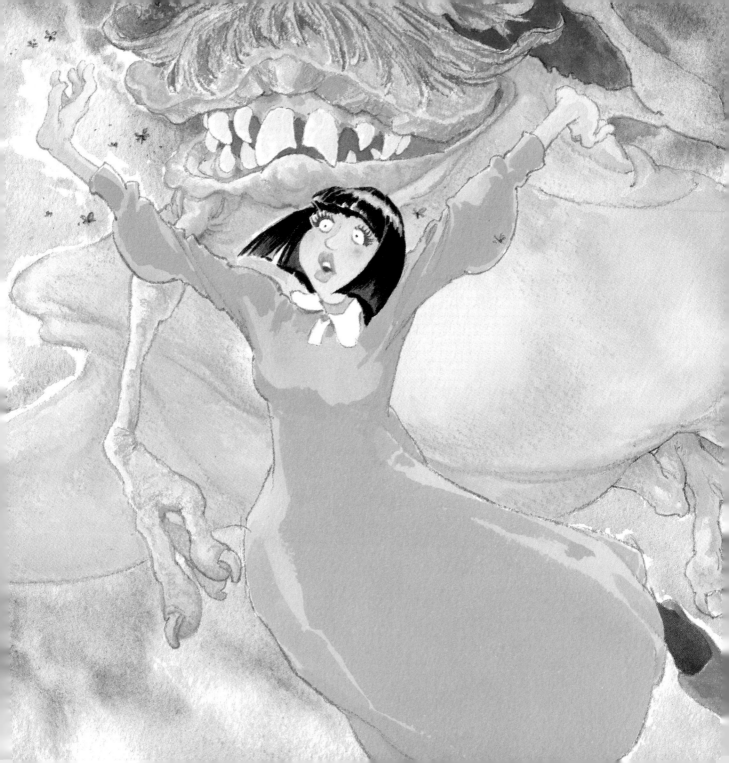

Carmen ran to the phone
and called the police.
She said, "Help, help! There is
a fart on top of Mommy
and Daddy."
"Don't be ridiculous," said the
police. "Good Canadians do
not have farts. What would
the Americans say?"

Nevertheless, three police drove
over to see what was going on.
They knocked on the door:
BLAM, BLAM, BLAM, BLAM.
Carmen opened the door
and said, "It's upstairs."

When the police were
halfway up the stairs,
the fart started
to jump on them.
They pulled out
their badges and
yelled,

But everyone knows that farts
don't listen to cops. It jumped on them.
They went, "Awk! Glach! Argggg!"
and fell right on down.

Carmen decided it was time to leave.
She was going to run completely away.

She ran through the livingroom,
through the kitchen into the backyard and . . .

crashed into her mother's favorite rose bush.

She got an idea. She picked the biggest rose and gave it a smell: MMMMMMM! Carmen held the rose out in front and walked back through the kitchen and into the livingroom.

She found the fart
hiding behind the piano
eating a can of beans.
Carmen walked up
and stuck the rose
in the fart's nose.

It said, "Awk! Glach! Argggg!

What a terrible smell!"
And it ran out
the front door.

Then the mother got up off the floor,
the father got up off the floor,
and the police got up off the floor.
They all looked at Carmen and yelled,
"THAT WAS A FART!"

"Don't be ridiculous," said Carmen.
"Good families like ours do not have farts."
And she walked up the stairs and went to bed.

But Carmen's mother stayed up very late
that night, working at her sewing machine,
and it turned out that sometimes . . .

. . . good children do have farts after all.